# THE SECRET GARDEN

Mary's Journal

www.harpercollinschildrens.com
ISBN 978-0-06-297104-3
Designed by Leslie Design
Art by Leslie Design
All paper textures, photo frames, and flower photos, used under license from Shutterstock.com.
20 21 22 23 24   PC   10 9 8 7 6 5 4 3 2 1
❖
First Edition

# THE SECRET GARDEN

# Mary's Journal

Written by Sia Dey

Based on the screenplay by Jack Thorne

Baesed on the original novel by Frances Hodgson Burnett

Art by Grant Montgomery and Leslie Design

Designed by Rick Farley and Leslie Design

**HARPER**

*An Imprint of HarperCollinsPublishers*

If you look the right way,
you can see that the whole world
is a garden.

I learned that everyone has a story to tell. This is my story . . . or rather, this is my journal about that story.

It's about a key, a secret,

botanical dreams,

an enchanted adventure,

a magical garden, and

how love grows.

This year, I learned something about life. Life can be like an empty garden. You can plant flowers all through a barren garden, but you can't just stand there and wait for them to grow. They never will. Gardens cannot grow on their own.

A garden needs love to grow.

- You need to care for it.
- Let it bask in the sun.
- Then let it drink the rain.
- Protect it from harm.

And before you know it, you'll see that
your garden isn't empty at all. That
maybe it never was. Before you, a
magical world grows, filled with flowers
of every shape and size and color.
Flowers and leaves, vines and thorns,
and roots. Thousands and thousands
of roots intertwining beneath your feet,
growing, living together as one.
And this beautiful garden of life began
with just a simple handful of seeds.

What would others do with such seeds,
I wonder. . . .

I have so much to say, but perhaps
I should start with my name.

My name is Mary Lennox.

and this is my story.

This is my story of

Fall. . . .

I like to tell stories, so I have decided to keep this journal.

My name is **Mary Lennox.**

I am ten years old.

I live in Punjab, India, and it's not been easy. It's quite hot, and my parents do not have much time for me. Daddy, busy with military duties, tries his best to play games with me. Our favorite one is hide-and-seek. He can never find me! Daddy says I am invisible. That means you cannot see me. This makes me think of Mother. Mother treats me like I am invisible.

My servant, or my ayah, looks after me most of the time.

She took this picture of me.

I was sad that day because I wanted to go outside and play.

Ayah also took this photo of Daddy and me. Mother wasn't around during this time.

My name is Mary Lennox, and I feel alone.

## Fall 1947, Tuesday

Yesterday Ayah told me I must stay indoors from now on. She wouldn't tell me why, but demanded I do not go outside for anything.

## Fall 1947, Wednesday

Today I woke up and my parents and Ayah were gone! Where did they go?

## Fall 1947, Friday

The sun has gone down. I'm a bit scared, but my doll Jemima reminded me to surround myself with my toys. She said they would make me safe.

Jemima makes me feel less lonely and bored.

## Fall 1947, Sunday

It's been several hours.

No one has come for me.

Jemima and I love telling stories, like this one. . . .

There were once two people called Mary and Jemima. They spent their days telling stories to each other. And then one day their mother and father were kidnapped by the evil demon Ravana, leaving them all alone.

Tomorrow I'll wake up to my family of toys all around me, with Jemima by my side.

My name is Mary Lennox, and Jemima still loves me.

Jemima and I took a nap today. We love taking naps! But today's nap was cut short by loud popping sounds outside.

I clutched Jemima, but the bangs continued.

BANG! BANG! BANG!

Again, and again, and again.

I wanted to look out the window, but Jemima told me not to.

Last night I heard footsteps on the streets just outside my window. I thought it might have been Daddy coming back for me. Or my mother, perhaps?

The footsteps grew louder and louder, until I heard them inside my home. Then at my bedroom door. That's when the soldiers found me.

I screamed!
But they told me they were good soldiers.
Maybe they were here to save me?

One soldier told me to pack only what I could carry. While looking for my coat, I overheard them talking about Daddy and Mother. Mother was sick with the disease that killed a lot of people. Daddy took Mother to the hospital, but she didn't make it through the night. Daddy was taken by the sickness as well.

My name is Mary Lennox,
and my heart is broken.

This is my story of

# Winter . . . .

My name is Mary Lennox, and I have no home.

I think about the times

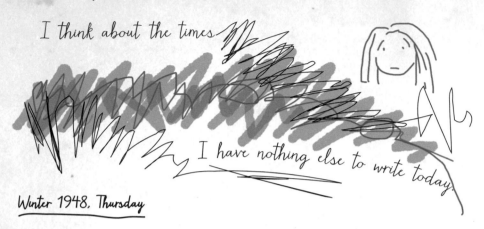

I have nothing else to write today.

Winter 1948, Thursday

It seems I have an uncle. He was married to my mother's twin sister, but she too died. He lives in England. I don't want to go to England to stay with a man I do not know! Why can't I just go back to India and live in my room with Jemima and drink tea and tell stories of princesses being saved by demons and monsters?

I guess Uncle and I have one thing in common, and it is not a good thing. We each lost people we loved.

Today Jemima and I were
taken to the docks to board a boat
headed for England. I could see
my reflection in the water below.
I noticed something different about myself.
Perhaps it was my dirty clothes or my uncombed hair.
Maybe it was my exhaustion or the heavy
feeling of sadness? No, I noticed I was no longer
a little girl. And only little girls have dolls.
I let Jemima go and watched as she
splashed into the waters below.

Then she was gone.

I have no more
tears left to cry,
and I hope to
never cry again.

My name is Mary Lennox, and
I am no longer a child.

## Winter 1948, Wednesday

Today an old, cranky woman met me at the docks of England. She told me her name was Mrs. Medlock and we were to board a train headed north. Well, those weren't her first words. Her first words were more of an insult, calling me a "plain little piece of goods." I think that means I am not very pretty? What an odd thing for a servant to say.

## Winter 1948, Friday

Mrs. Medlock has proven to be quite the rigid one. Below is a list of rules and demands I must follow while at Uncle's home.

- Do not expect any luxury while at Uncle's home
- I was informed what rooms I could enter and what rooms I must keep out of
- For now, I am confined to just one room: my room
- I am not to wander about
- I am to stay in my room until I am told otherwise
- I am to mind my own business
- There is no one to talk to, but I am not to go looking for someone to talk to
- And no exploring and no poking about

Poking about? Am I dog? How dare she!

Just when I thought she was finished with her rules, she started in on the rules involving my uncle, whom I have yet to meet, by the way.

- Stay clear of my uncle

- If I do see my uncle, leave him be

- When he speaks to me, I reply with Sir

- He may stare at me, but I am not to stare at him

- Say nothing fancy

- He has many concerns and doesn't need me to add to his list

Mrs. Medlock said something strange while on the train. Well, all of it was strange, but this was really strange. She said Uncle has "suffered enough" and that I should remain a "shadow" because of how I look. Being a shadow shouldn't be difficult. I am used to being invisible.

## Winter 1948, Saturday

We arrived at Uncle's home. And it wasn't a home at all. It was a mansion. The Misselthwaite Manor. It was like a small city! It reminds me of a castle from one of my stories. But this castle has not been cared for in a very long time. It is dark and gloomy. It even has sections that are crumbling.

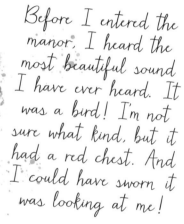

Before I entered the manor, I heard the most beautiful sound I have ever heard. It was a bird! I'm not sure what kind, but it had a red chest. And I could have sworn it was looking at me!

## Winter 1948, Monday

I found this drawing under a cabinet by my room. Mrs. Medlock didn't see me pick it up.
It looks like the mansion.
    Even sad like the mansion.

My name is Mary Lennox, and I feel sorry for this broken house.

After more rules and demands from Medlock, I finally arrived at a massive bedroom. Mrs. Medlock let me in, then turned and left, shutting the door behind her.

This wasn't a home. It was a prison.

Why do I feel so alone?

Nothing was familiar to me and everything felt cold. The bed was hard and there was no color anywhere. It was filled with blacks and grays. If loneliness was a color, it would be this room.

Except for the wallpaper. On it was a pattern of a tree with leaves and a small bird (she didn't have a red chest). I tore a piece off that had come undone in a corner and decided to keep it for my journal.

Oh, how I wish I was back in India with Jemima telling stories about Rama and Sita.

I just had another nightmare.

It was a beautiful day in India, and I was in a garden. The garden was full of beautiful flowers of all colors and they smelled so fresh. It felt so real, this dream, but I knew it couldn't be. When I walked by the flowers in the garden, they moved with me, trying to reach out and grab me.

Then I saw Mother. I know it. I didn't see Daddy, which made me sad. I climbed a nearby tree and yelled her name, but Mother just walked away. Perhaps sound does not exist in dreams.

As I sit here and write this, I feel there is something here, in this room with me, right now. . . .

A ghost perhaps?

No, ghosts aren't real.
Neither is magic or monsters.

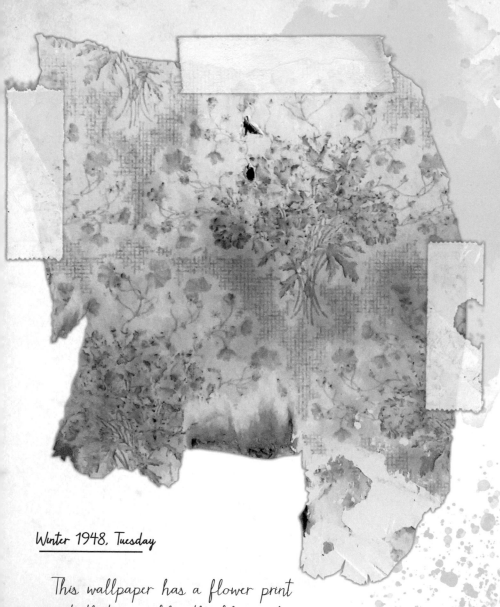

Winter 1948, Tuesday

This wallpaper has a flower print
on it that resembles the blooms from
my dream. I tore a tiny piece off
and keep it here to remind me of a
happier time spent with Mother.

The maids in England
are by far
the rudest in the world!

I met an interesting person today—
Martha—she is a maid. Very young.
Somewhat pretty. OK, she is fairly pretty.
But nonetheless, a maid. I asked her for
things that I needed, but she seemed far
more interested in getting to know me than
serving me. How odd is that!

Martha spoke of spring approaching.
Which reminded me that perhaps
everything around me is dead and gone
because the winter has taken it away. Yes,
this seems to be all winter's fault.

Martha mentioned something of interest. She has a brother.
His name is Dickon, and he spends his days out on the hills
around the manor. But doing what, I wonder? Perhaps he may
know something about those cries I heard the other night.

My name is Mary Lennox,
and I shall find out.

I've been making some very strange observations indeed at Misselthwaite Manor. . . .
I overheard Mrs. Medlock talking outside my window. I peeked out and saw an old man with a hunchback dragging a bed to the front gates. As if that wasn't strange enough, he seems to have dragged a

lot of beds. Why on earth would anyone be dragging beds outside? Whatever the reason, Mrs. Medlock tried to stop him, but he was determined. And apparently very thirsty. He kept drinking from a small canteen he kept in his back pocket. It must not have tasted good. With every sip, his face puckered up like he was sucking on a lemon. Who is this man?
The man is my uncle, Archibald. Mrs. Medlock just yelled his name.

More on Uncle and his strange behavior.

Wandering around the manor, I saw Uncle and Medlock carrying things into a room near a grand staircase. The room was a massive library with space for thousands of books! It was bigger than any library I had ever seen in India. But this was a library no more. . . .

Almost all of the books were gone, and it was now being used as a room for storage.

I did manage to grab a few books that were lying on the floor. The rest of the room was chaotically stacked with chairs, tables, sketches and paintings of flowers and courtyards . . . and all of it covered with dust. Lots of dust. Dust so thick it was hard to see what was hiding underneath it.

That's when I heard the voices. . . .

Inside the library, Medlock and Uncle were sorting through pictures and quarreling over the importance of them. Uncle wanted to rid the room of everything, throw it away, even burn it. Mrs. Medlock attempted to persuade him otherwise, but it was no use. Uncle was adamant.

That is, until Medlock held up a painting of a woman. I could not make out the features very well, but she was quite elegant and beautiful. And somewhat familiar . . .

But my uncle's face when he saw this woman!
Underneath my uncle's anger and annoyance was
something all too familiar—a broken heart.

This was not the time to contemplate
such a matter. I thought of those
books and how they should not
go to waste, nor should the pile
of sketches. I quickly grabbed one
that caught my eye. It looked like
a gate to someplace special. Is it
here at Uncle's manor?

I am making a note for myself
to come back later tonight and
collect the following:

✔ Books
✔ Pencil drawings
✔ Colored pencils
✔ Paint brushes
✔ Watercolor painter's set
✔ Tape

they were on
the third shelf
to the left

Walking the halls I heard a scream. But from who?

My name is Mary Lennox,
and I have more rooms to explore.

There is something beyond the manor.
I'm sure of it. . . .

While skipping in the woods today, I encountered the first sign of life outside the halls of Misselthwaite—next to the red-chested bird, who I will continue to swear was looking right at me! Also, I now know the bird is a robin based on the *BIRDS OF BRITAIN* book that I "borrowed" from the library.

I was sitting on a tree trunk eating a sandwich when out of the woods came a small dog! It was filthy and desperately needed grooming, but a dog, nonetheless.

The dog and I stared at one another, or rather, we shared a moment. Its eyes were soft. And familiar. It sounds odd, even as I write this. Finally, it turned and ran into woods.

That's when I remembered! In another room in the main hallway, I found what I am calling the picture room. Inside were dozens of photos scattered all over the floor, the desk, in piles by the fireplace, everywhere!

Here's a photo of a dog.

It must be the same dog!

I've decided to call her Jemima.
My friend, Jemima.

This place is becoming more
and more like a prison. All I
want to do is run free like the
dog from the woods and roam
as I please, but how can I?

I want to
be like the birds
on the wallpaper in
my room. To be able to fly
high above everything . . .

## Winter 1948, Tuesday

The screams woke me up again. No one seems to know what they are. Nonsense.

Someone knows something.

## Winter 1948, Wednesday

Martha and I had an argument.

I told her I did not ask to be here, that I did not want to leave India. She said that my uncle did not ask to take me in, but here I am.

I cannot help but think that there is something much deeper happening here.

- Uncle Archibald and why his heart is broken
- The manor (or estate) and why it died
- The woman in the portrait and her relation to Uncle
- The screams at night
- The property and what's beyond the hills
- The dog who lives in the woods

I do not know why I'm here, but I need to find out.

My name is Mary Lennox,
and I have so much to say!

Tonight proved to be the most interesting
and rewarding night thus far since arriving
at Misselthwaite.

The screams woke me again, and this time I would
not go back to sleep until I found out just what
they were and where they were coming from.

I followed them down the corridor, around a corner,
and down a hall to a room I was sure was the home
of the screams and cries. I peeked inside and there it
was . . . a boy.

He was about my age. He lay there, lifeless. I
couldn't move. I couldn't scream. I just stood there
in fear. It was a ghost, I was sure of it! Then he
opened his eyes, and I ducked out of sight.

But he saw me. I told him my name was Mary
Lennox and I was ten years old, that my mother
was the sister to Uncle's wife. The boy looked at me
oddly, then told me that the uncle I speak of was
his father!

We were cousins!

I never knew I had a cousin! His name was Colin, and he was a self-righteous little lord if I have ever seen one! He called me thin, and said I smiled with no teeth. So I told him that he was very pale and didn't seem to smile at all.

We stared at one another for a moment then we laughed, and for the first time in a long time I felt good!

I had so many questions. I asked if the house was cursed, and he said yes, that it killed his mother and tried to kill him too.

Seems like we both had known tragedy.
It also seemed something was growing around me.

Family.

Speaking of family . . .

After what has felt like weeks, I finally met my uncle. Archibald Craven.

Here's a picture I found in his study. I doubt he'll miss it.

There was also a picture on Uncle's desk of Colin and I assume Colin's mother, Grace. My mother's sister. There was something so familiar about her. It's the woman from the painting!

He made it clear he did not want me to be in here. However, he said if I do not give him trouble, he would permit me to stay.

This fell heavy on me. For the first time, I realized I actually want to be here!

Something inside me wants to grow. And so I must . . .

. . . and I know just WHERE to start.

This is my story of a

Garden . . . .

<u>Spring 1948, Wednesday</u>

I met my dog friend, Jemima, at our usual spot, and we had lunch together, sharing a sandwich that she very much enjoyed. And then I saw him. From the corner of my eye, there was a boy. I know Martha has a brother and perhaps this might be him? He started to run, but I couldn't let him get away without asking who he was. Jemima and I gave chase into the woods, but we lost him.

And that's when I heard a horrible cry! It was Jemima! Her foot was caught in a trap. I was so scared and so was she. Jemima ran and I followed her, trying to free her leg from the trap. With all my might I finally got her free. And Jemima hopped her way deeper into the forest and crawled under a large wall covered in the greenest ivy I have ever seen. There was no way I would make it under.

So I went over.

And that's when I discovered something magical. . . .

It was unlike anything I have ever seen before. I found a world filled with wild and overgrown shapes. Everywhere I turned, there were petrified roots and trunks, as if they had exploded in one direction and then another. As if they were part of a war that had once occurred here.

That's when I heard Jemima.

There, across a stream, her coat all wet,
sat Jemima, her injured leg underneath
her. She looked so sad and in pain.

But I couldn't get to her. We were separated by a
stream, this beautiful flowing stream of water. And it was
bubbling. Who had ever seen such a thing? Was it hot?
To get to Jemima, I would have to find out. I took
off my coat and slowly stepped into the water. I
discovered it wasn't hot at all. No, instead it was
cold as ice. But I didn't care. Deeper into the
stream I went until I could not feel the
dirt between my toes. Thank goodness
Ayah taught me how to swim.

I finally made it to Jemima. I approached her, but she was scared. And I was shivering. We needed each other.

We needed to find something that would help us, and so we headed deeper into this . . . place.

I was filled with happiness being here. I felt so good I barked into the air! And then Jemima barked too! Then she ran into the ankle-deep waters and I jumped in too. And we splashed together, her barking and me laughing!

Jemima and I ran past these beautiful giant ferns, through a grove of strange trees with massive trunks and roots growing everywhere. I have never seen anything like this! There before us was a sunken temple. It was ancient looking and had no roof. Who lived here? A king? A queen? A wizard?

Spring 1948, Thursday

I went back to the sunken temple again. The pool of water was cold. But every time I step into it, I get this feeling of happiness inside. It is like this water is healing my soul.

Spring 1948, Friday

Whenever I went back, this magical place
was full of deep browns, greens, and grays,
scattered with occasional reds from winter roses
and strange, mutated mushrooms and fungi.

The botany books I have been reading describe places
like this, where all plant life lives together, mingling,
growing, and dying as one element.

But nothing is dying within these woods. Not that I can see. Yes, it may be full of leaves that have fallen from the trees, but they are not decayed in any manner.

They are full of life. But how?

## Leaves and Nuts

Some of the sketches from the picture room have the very same leaves I saw in the garden.

Like this one.

And this one.

I shall discover their names as I continue to study these little wonders.

And even more to write about . . .

I found a special key!

It was given to me by a beautiful red robin. Well, not literally, but the robin led me to this key.

In *BIRDS OF BRITAIN*, page 38, I found a drawing of a robin.

A few things I learned about robins:

 Robins are considered to be an indicator of the coming spring season.

 They have a lifespan of two years! Who would believe such a short time for such a beautiful creature?

 The first British postmen wore red coats, so people nicknamed them "robin" or "redbreast."

I followed the robin to a stone-faced pillar with a huge cavity on its side. And to my surprise, what did I find inside?

# This key!

If someone can draw a robin, I can draw a key!

OK, it's not the best drawing I've done lately. The detail on the key makes it very special, I'm certain. But what is it for?

# Ivy

Flowers do not say how they feel. They do not whine about what they want. They just are. Take for example the ivy vines that grow like veins across buildings, trees, and rocks. You must appreciate the beauty of this. The ivy does not smother what it grows on. It gives it another layer of life. It's like they live together as one.

The Hedera, commonly called ivy, represents eternity, fidelity, and strong, affectionate attachment, such as wedded love and friendship, and has great spiritual significance.

In ancient Greece, wreaths of ivy were used to crown victorious athletes.

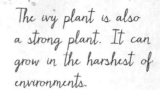

The ivy plant is also a strong plant. It can grow in the harshest of environments.

I think if I were a plant, I might be ivy. . . .

My name is Mary Lennox, and I am like ivy. . . .

# Hazel

I've read a section on the hazel tree, which can also be a shrub. It's said that hazel is linked to wisdom and inspiration!

I believe Martha is like a hazel tree. But I don't eat her fruit. I eat her porridge. Which is starting to grow on me.

Hazel

Spring 1948, Sunday

I met Martha's brother, Dickon. While looking for Jemima, I saw him by the moors. He tried to run again, but I was faster! I threatened to tell Martha about what his horrible trap did to Jemima. That's when Dickon said Jemima was a HE! Yes! Jemima is a boy!

Dickon said he could heal ~~Jemima~~ the dog. I didn't trust Dickon at first. But there was a look in his eyes. He reminded me of my father. He meant it. But can I trust him to keep a secret?

The answer was spit. Spit and a handshake seemed to mean the world when it came to keeping secrets and making promises. We spat on our hands and shook. A bond forever. He would never tell. And so, off we went to help the dog who needs a name! For now, Dog will do.

When Dickon climbed that wall and saw the garden, he could not speak. Only stare in amazement! I smiled.

But his excitement left. He spotted ~~Jemima~~ **the dog**. He looked worse. Dickon carried him to the stream and washed the poor dog's leg as he cried and howled. We wrapped his leg and stepped back as the dog tried to walk.

And then . . . something . . . happened.
Something I cannot explain.

The grass around ~~Jemima~~ **the dog** began to grow up his leg and around his body like a cocoon. It wouldn't let him go!

I screamed at Dickon to do something. "Give it time," he said. Tomorrow we would have our answer.

So here I am, in my room, writing and hoping.
Hoping . . .

## Spring 1948, Monday

The garden had cured Jemima Dog! Before we could celebrate, the spring air spoke to us. Dickon and I stumbled upon an iron gate covered in vines, and behind the vines a keyhole.
The garden wanted us to find this!

And I had a key! THE key!

But something was missing. Colin . . .

We MUST get Colin!

We raced back to the manor and snuck into Colin's room. We burst in and into his chair he went, utterly speechless. We pushed him down the corridor and out the manor. We raced him across the field and toward the ivy wall. I could see Colin grip his wheelchair.

I ran faster and faster, pushing poor Colin, who was dying from air (not really). He screamed and cried out as we "hit" the wall.

Then everything changed for him. . . .

What we have discovered is a magical place. Colin, Dickon, Dog, myself . . .

It was wondrous. Beautiful, bright, living colors surrounded us. It felt like they went on forever. It was as if a rainbow had fallen from the sky and landed before me.

How could this be? We didn't know and didn't care—we only cared how this made us FEEL. We were happy. We were laughing. We felt loved.

My name is Mary Lennox, and my heart sings.

Spring 1948, Thursday

We were greeted by a canopy of the
brightest yellow laburnum flowers I
have ever seen. They were not below us
in a garden bed. They were above us,
forming a tunnel. And we followed this
tunnel, never taking our eyes off of the
yellow above us. All four of us.
Jemima, Dickon, myself,
and now with Colin . . .

# Daffodil

Daffodil

Spring 1948, Friday

They say the daffodil is
a gift that will ensure
happiness. But always
remember to present
daffodils in a bunch.
Well, here we are.

My name is Mary Lennox,
and these are my friends.

I have more to write! I lay in the grass, surrounded by the most beautiful colors. It felt surreal. The stone pillars and columns behind me looked like a drawing I found a photo of in the picture room, which means someone was tending to this place! I was surrounded by a riot of reds—scarlet willow and red-barked dogwood and bed after bed of strange red flowers, which I now know are poinsettias, based on this picture I found in the botany book.

The Christmas Flower

# Poinsettia

It's said that poinsettias' association with Christmas comes from a Mexican legend. A child, with no means for a grander gift, gathered humble weeds from the side of the road to place at the church on Christmas Eve. The congregation watched as the weeds turned into brilliant red and green flowers.
A Christmas Miracle.

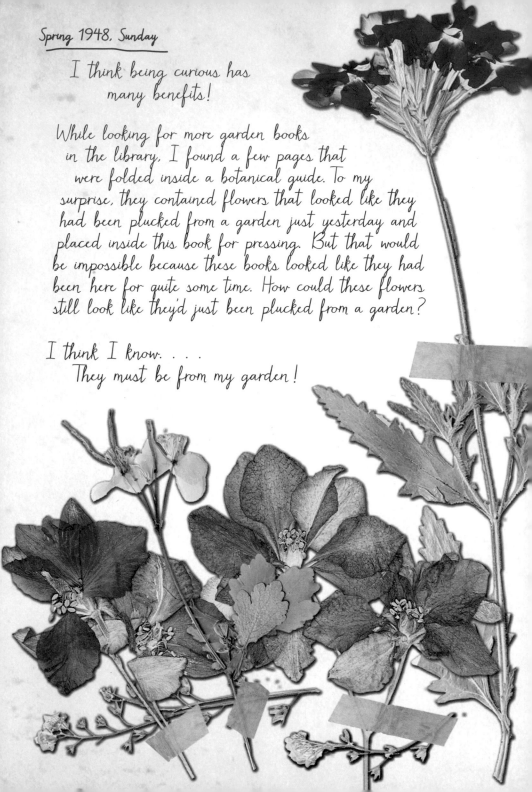

Spring 1948, Sunday

I think being curious has
    many benefits!

While looking for more garden books
  in the library, I found a few pages that
    were folded inside a botanical guide. To my
  surprise, they contained flowers that looked like they
  had been plucked from a garden just yesterday and
  placed inside this book for pressing. But that would
  be impossible because these books looked like they had
  been here for quite some time. How could these flowers
  still look like they'd just been plucked from a garden?

I think I know. . . .
    They must be from my garden!

I have decided, with such a beautiful garden to explore,
I shall now keep a botanical journal. I want to learn
as much as possible, because this place is so full of
love and life and magic and wonder that everyone must
know about it. But as I write this, I realize that may
not be the best idea. For it would no longer be my
secret place. It could be trampled and destroyed by
people from all over. I must think about this carefully.
If Mrs. Medlock discovered what I was doing, it
would be the end of the garden, and the end of my
time here at Misselthwaite Manor.

The key to picking the right flower is the freshness of its petals. A strong stem will also add longevity to its survival within your journal.

The best time to pick flowers is just after the sun rises, when all the dew has been evaporated by the sun's rays.

When plucked, cut away most of the leaves.

**Petal**

**Flower**

**Leaf**

**Stem**

**Bud**

**Shoot**

You'll want to dip the flower into water, giving it a nice bath to help rinse off any dirt or other debris.

Now lay the flat face of the flower within the pages of an old book, and you are ready to press.

Close the book on the flower and place some heavier books on top to weigh the bottom one down.

Be sure not to disturb the
arrangement of the flowers upon
closing! After a few days, open
the book and remove the flowers.

Place them in your floral
journal on a clean sheet of
paper. Hold them in place
using sticky tape. Now you
are ready to write to the
world about this wonderful
floral piece!

The floral guide calls
people that study
flowers botanists.

Botany is the study of plants.

My name is Mary Lennox,
and I am a botanist!

I have discovered a secret garden, and now I have discovered a secret room!

While hiding from Mrs. Medlock, I stumbled into a large room with beautiful paintings and furniture and little trinkets of all sorts! Everything was so exotic! There were beautiful murals and a wooden chest with little flowers carved in it.

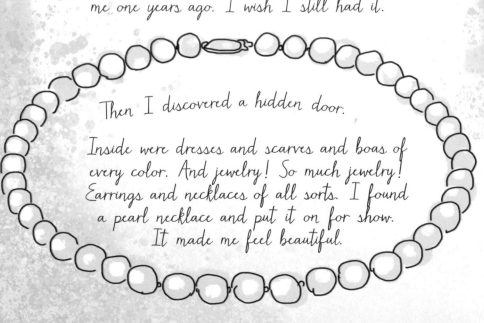

I saw an elephant carved from black wood. I remember these elephants from Punjab. Mother gave me one years ago. I wish I still had it.

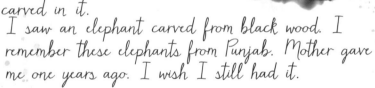

Then I discovered a hidden door.

Inside were dresses and scarves and boas of every color. And jewelry! So much jewelry! Earrings and necklaces of all sorts. I found a pearl necklace and put it on for show. It made me feel beautiful.

I've been looking through the secret room for some time
now and have found so many wonderful pictures!

Pictures of the garden when it was alive. Pictures of a
swing under a very large tree. Tomorrow, Dickon, Colin,
and I will look for this.

Even more pictures!
Pictures of my mother and her sister!
But who are those children?
Could it be Colin and me?

I have to go! If Mrs. Medlock finds me,
I will definitely be sent to that all-girls school.

## Spring 1948, Tuesday

I saw these things
growing on rocks and
trees in the garden. They
were yellow and blue
and green. Are they
killing the trees? Are
they killing the garden?
I hope not. . . .

## Spring 1948, Thursday

Lichens are not killing the
trees! They are, however, telling
something about the trees' health.
THE BOTANICAL FLORAS
AND FAUNAS book says
lichen is considered to be a type
of fungus, but it provides support
and protection.
So it mustn't be that bad.

This reminds me of Mrs. Medlock and her
relationship with Uncle! Not that she's a fungus
or that she's killing things, or Uncle . . . but she
keeps him going. She helps him exist. But I do not
think she provides good air quality. She is quite stale
at times in her aroma. I'm sure a simple soaking in
bath salts would do the trick.

Spring 1948, Friday

This was the plant I saw when I first entered the garden. I remember its beautiful huge umbrella-like leaves that were towering over my head! They could have been trees!

I think I saw a Gunnera plant in Uncle's office. They are also called clover flowers. When they're young, they are bright and hold themselves upward so that visiting pollinators such as small bees can easily see them.

Spring 1948, Saturday

I took some grass for my journal. But this is not normal grass. It's special. It came to life and wrapped itself around Jemima's injured leg like a green blanket.

Spring 1948, Monday

# Magnolias

Magnolias are believed to be one of the first flowering plants to evolve on Earth. In ancient China, magnolias were thought to be the perfect symbols of womanly beauty and gentleness. I would agree to that!

Although magnolias are mostly seen with white petals, some come in pink, yellow, or purple and have very interesting meanings.

**White** stands for the moon and for spells cast on Mondays.

**Yellow**: is for the sun and for spells cast on Sundays.

**Pink** represents friendship and love. Spells using pink flowers are best cast on Friday.

**Purple**: This color has stood for royalty since Roman times.

## Magnolia

It seems Colin is deathly afraid of flowers. Just look at this terror of a rose. Colin thinks the stench of roses will kill him . . . silly boy!

# Roses

The smell of fresh roses is heavenly!

And the colors of roses! Roses can be found in shades of white, yellow, pink, orange, and red. But there are no such things as blue or black roses. They do not exist, but maybe in a magic garden, I shall find one!

I've looked for over an hour and still have not found a black or blue rose. While I took a break, I read that roses symbolize certain values.

A **red** rose is a symbol of love.

A **yellow** rose is a symbol of friendship.

An **orange** rose is a symbol of enthusiasm.

A **white** rose is a symbol of purity.

A **pink** rose is a symbol of joy.

# Azalea

The azalea flower is a symbol of femininity and softness. It is something that you would give a loved one. The symbolic meaning of this flower tells loved ones to take care of themselves.

Azaleas come in all kinds of great colors. Some of them are white, some yellow, some pink, some purple, among many other colors.

## Blue Azalea

The azalea tends to represent good qualities of personalities, but it also symbolizes specific emotions or events.

- Taking care of yourself and your family

- Elegance and wealth

- Remembering your home with fondness or wishing to return to it

- Passion that is still developing and fragile

- Femininity and beauty

## Azalea

My name is Mary Lennox, and my mother was an azalea.

I'm getting better at my painting! I lightly painted this image of the magic water castle. That's what I call it. If you touch the water there, it will heal you. Especially on the inside.

# Rhododendron

The rhododendron flower, another favorite of mine!

In 1834 the American poet and essayist Ralph Waldo Emerson wrote a poem titled "The Rhodora, On Being Asked, Whence Is the Flower." I saw this in Uncle's study and shall borrow it when I return home.

The rhododendron is the national flower of Nepal, where the flower is considered edible and enjoyed for its sour taste. I'm going to dare Colin, or Dickon to eat one!

The camellia is native to China, where it has a rich national history, particularly in the southwest region. The camellia is also a highly respected flower in Japan and is often referred to as the Japanese rose.

Camellia

Generally camellia flowers represent love, affection, and admiration. Camellia flowers bloom in white, pink, and red, and each color has its own unique symbolism.

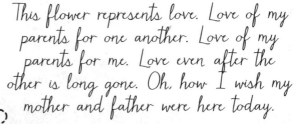

This flower represents love. Love of my parents for one another. Love of my parents for me. Love even after the other is long gone. Oh, how I wish my mother and father were here today.

I have picked two camellias to represent my parents, who will live in this journal forever.

# Hibiscus

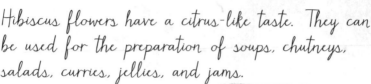

I found these facts about the hibiscus flower fascinating!

Hibiscus is known as "shoe flower" in China because people use hibiscus to polish their shoes.

Hibiscus flowers have a citrus-like taste. They can be used for the preparation of soups, chutneys, salads, curries, jellies, and jams.

## Hibiscus

Tori, my friend from Punjab, would always have a fresh hibiscus flower by her ear. She said she was saving it for when she was hungry.

# Hydrangea

First discovered in Japan, the name hydrangea
roughly translates to "water barrel," referring to
the hydrangea's need for plenty of water and
its cup-shaped flowers. With its wooden stems
and lacy flowers packed closely together in
a pom-pom, the hydrangea's color ranges from
white to blue to pink to purple.

Common color meanings for hydrangeas include:

**Pink**—linked to romance, heartfelt
emotions, love, weddings, and marriage

**Blue**—connected to frigidity, asking
for forgiveness, and expressing regret

**White**—known as a symbol of purity, grace,
abundance, and bragging or boasting

**Purple**—used to indicate a desire for a
deeper understanding of someone else or to
symbolize abundance and wealth

There remains some debate over the hydrangea's symbolism—with some connecting it to vanity and boastfulness (perhaps reflecting its abundance of petals and lavish, rounded shape) and others suggesting that a bouquet of hydrangea expresses the giver's gratefulness for the recipient's understanding. Still others suggest it represents anything that's sincerely heartfelt.

## Hydrangea

- Heartfelt and honest emotions of any kind

- Gratitude and thanksgiving to someone else

- Developing a deeper understanding between two people

- Grace and beauty, sometimes taken to the extremes of vanity and narcissism

- Heartlessness and acting without thinking about the feelings of another

Colin is definitely a hydrangea!
And perhaps Uncle . . . For all of the above reasons.

# Dandelion

## Dandelion

Colin picked a dandelion flower today and held it up to the blue sky. We watched as the tiny seeds broke off and flew through the air, swirling and winding, blowing wherever the winds took them. Will they ever come back?

Once dandelions turn
from their vibrant yellow
color to their white/gray
seed, they can be blown,
sending the seeds into
the air.

While some people may blow
these flowers for more superstitious reasons,
people also blow dandelions for their visual appeal.
I like both reasons. The dried seeds shimmer in the
air, especially when it's sunny.

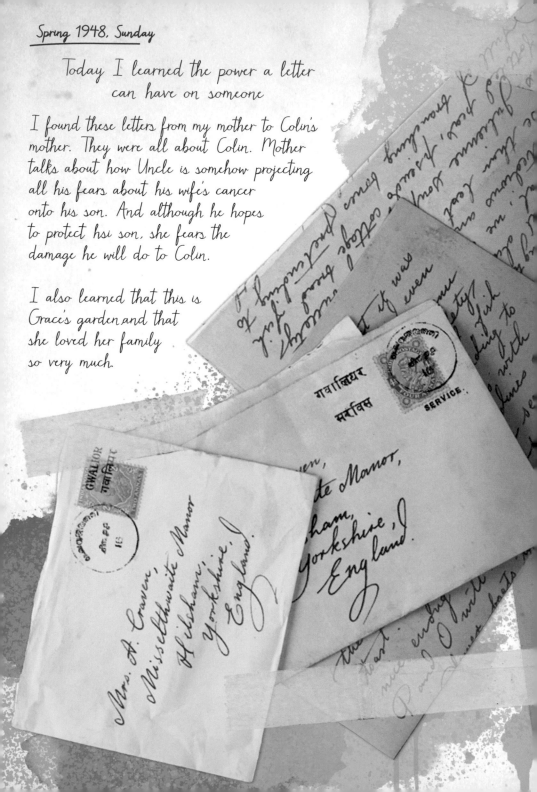

Spring 1948, Sunday

Today I learned the power a letter
can have on someone

I found these letters from my mother to Colin's
mother. They were all about Colin. Mother
talks about how Uncle is somehow projecting
all his fears about his wife's cancer
onto his son. And although he hopes
to protect hsi son, she fears the
damage he will do to Colin.

I also learned that this is
Grace's garden and that
she loved her family
so very much.

<u>Spring. 1948. Monday</u>

Dear Mary,

Reminding myself
to practice with
Dickon. Every day
we will sit and
read together until
he is all caught up
on his words.

June 21st

...racie,

How lovely to
...news. I am so
...that you are enjoying
...he gardens at
Misselthwaite

the man
& pala

I shall it be lovely
...he spring
...opening opening
...exciting planning
...ich summer flowers
...ou will put in the border

We do have hollyhocks and
Michaelmas daisies here too
as well as roses.

Perhaps you could send out some packets
of Suttons seeds and I will have them
sown so that I can see them when they
flower from the veranda and think of you. I'm glad that
Colin is being taken out in his pram in
the garden I hope that he enjoys it and
being outside gives him a better appetite.
Well, we are back from the hills
where we have been since March.
It is such an effort to leave even though the

Mrs. A. Craven,
Misselthwaite Manor,
Hilsham,
Yorkshire,
England

Colin read letter after letter that my
mother wrote . . .and they were about me.

# My mother loved me!

My favorite letter said this:

She's bold and slightly dangerous, and she has a spirit
that nothing can quench. I'd be scared for her if
I wasn't so proud of her!

Letters are memories.

My name is Mary Lennox, and the only memories of my mother
I can hold are these letters.

I wish I could have bottled up every laugh, every smile, every tear,
every drop of love that fell onto my heart. I'd plant seeds of every
flower I could find and then I would open these bottles of memories
that we shared. And I would wait. I would wait until you grew
back into my life. Yes.
This is how I would get you back and make
you more than just a memory.

What is a family?

I did not know before I came
to Misselthwaite Manor.
I knew it consisted of a mother,
a father, and their children. But I know
now it is much more than that. It is everyone
around you that you love and that loves you.
And they come from every walk of life. They
come in every color. Every shape. Everything
different. Yet we share a bond that cannot
be broken. We are a family, and a family
cannot be broken. We are a garden of every
flower growing and living together as one.
Our roots are deep, and together we create a
bond that cannot be broken. Even when one
falls or wilts, we are there to guide them back.
Push them in the right direction. Never give up
even when they want to give up on themselves.
We show them we are there for them.

With a smile.

With trust. With hugs. With tears.

With love.

My dearest niece—

Thank you. Thank you for bringing my son back to me and me back to my son. What you have done is nothing short of a miracle. You have given me another chance in life and have reminded me to love all the things that I hold dear, even the ones right in front of me. Before you brought this magical garden back to life, it was hurting inside. And so was I. But because of you, I shall grow and the love for my son shall grow as well. Thank you for planting a seed inside me.

With love, from your not-so-grumpy uncle,

Archibald

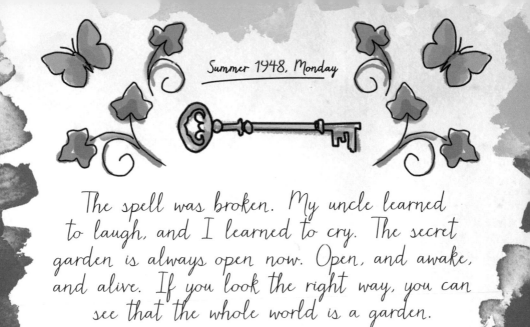

The spell was broken. My uncle learned to laugh, and I learned to cry. The secret garden is always open now. Open, and awake, and alive. If you look the right way, you can see that the whole world is a garden.

I cannot tell you what will happen when this book closes. But what I can tell you is that I hope these words live past the last page. And that wherever we go, and whatever we do, we live within one another and help one another grow. And if so, we will never be apart. For we all live in the Garden of Love. Just hold your hand over your heart and feel it. Growing. Beating. Alive. That's you. That's me. That's us. Forever in our garden.

We all have a story. . . .

What's yours?